WHEN THE WIND STOPS

by

Charlotte Zolotow

Illustrated by Joe Lasker

"Where does the sun go when the day ends?" asked the little boy as his mother tucked him into bed. "The day doesn't end, it only begins somewhere else. The sun will rise there, when the night begins here. Nothing ends. It only begins in another place or in a different way." So the boy kept asking questions: "Where does the rain go, where do the waves go, where does the road go?" Can your mother answer all these questions, too?

K

Classification and Dewey Decimal: Easy (E)

About the Author:

CHARLOTTE ZOLOTOW attended the University of Wisconsin. She came to New York and worked in the children's book department of a publishing company. She married Maurice Zolotow, the writer, and began writing children's books. Her writing mirrors the freshness and wonder of a child's vision.

Mrs. Zolotow enjoys gardening and is the mother of two children. She lives in Hastings-on-Hudson, New York, and has returned to editing books for young people.

About the Illustrator:

JOE LASKER has taught art and has had many exhibitions of his paintings, which are sensitive and imaginative. Mr. Lasker lives in Norwalk, Conn., with his wife and three children.

when
the wind
stops

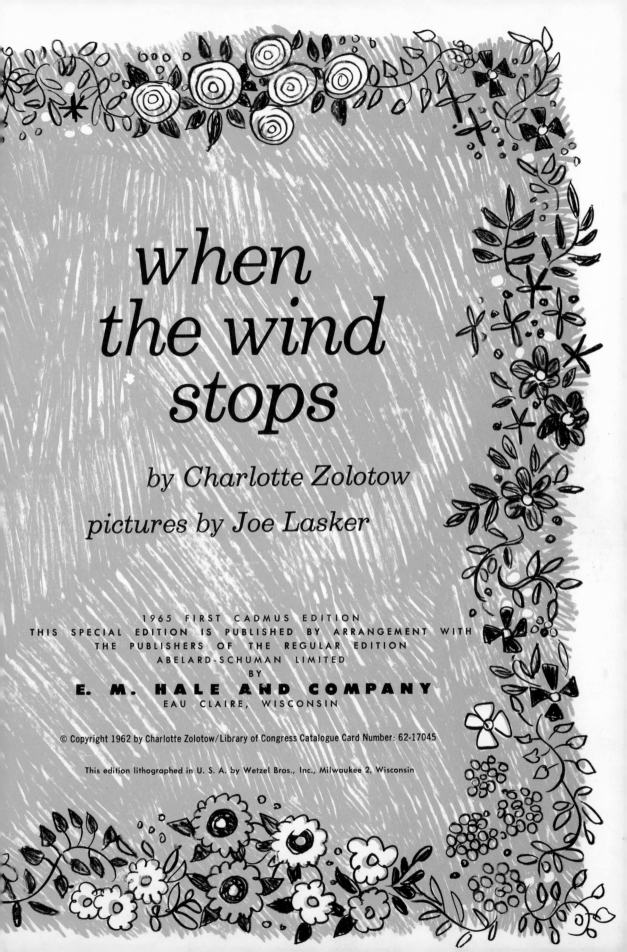

when the wind stops

by Charlotte Zolotow

pictures by Joe Lasker

1965 FIRST CADMUS EDITION
THIS SPECIAL EDITION IS PUBLISHED BY ARRANGEMENT WITH
THE PUBLISHERS OF THE REGULAR EDITION
ABELARD-SCHUMAN LIMITED
BY

E. M. HALE AND COMPANY
EAU CLAIRE, WISCONSIN

This edition lithographed in U. S. A. by Wetzel Bros., Inc., Milwaukee 2, Wisconsin

The great bright yellow sun had shone all
day and now the day was coming to an end.
The light in the sky changed from blue to
pink to a strange dusky purple, as the sun
sank lower into the long glowing clouds.
The little boy was sorry to see the day end.

It had been a good one.
He and his friend had played in the garden.
When they were tired of playing they lay down
in the grass and felt the sun on them,
warm and soft, like a sleepy cat resting.

There had been icy lemonade in
the afternoon which they drank
sitting under the pear tree.
And the little boy's father had
read him a story on the porch
before he went to bed.

Now his mother had come to tuck him in.
"Why does the day have to end?" he asked her.
"So night can begin," she said. "Look out
there," and she pointed away from the sinking
sun to where, high in the darkening sky,
behind the branches of the pear tree,
the little boy could see a pale sliver of moon.
"That is the night beginning," his mother
said resting her hand on his shoulder, "the night
with moon and stars and darkness and quiet—
for you to have sweet dreams in."

"But where is the sun going?" asked the
little boy. "Where does it go when the day ends?"
"The day doesn't end," said his mother. "It
only begins somewhere else. The sun will
rise there, when the night begins here.
Nothing ends. It only begins in another
place or in a different way."

"Everything?" asked the little boy.
"Everything," said his mother.

The little boy got back into his bed and
his mother sat down beside him.
"Where does the wind go when it stops?"
he asked.

"It blows away to make the trees dance
somewhere else."

"Where does the flame go when the candle burns out?"

"Into the air for new fires."

"Where does the dandelion fluff go
when it blows away?"

"It carries the seed for new dandelions
to someone else's lawn."

"Where does the road go when it gets out of sight?"

"It leads to another little boy who sees it begin in the distance."

"Where does the mountain go
when you reach the top?"

"Down to the valley
for someone there to climb."

"Where do the waves go when they break on the shore?"

"Back over the sand to the sea to become new waves again."

"Where does the ship go when it sails from port?"

"Over the horizon to a country far away."

"Where does the rain go when the storm is over?"

"Into the clouds to make another storm."

"Where do the clouds go when they move across the sky?"

"To make shade somewhere else."

"Where does the train go when the tunnel
swallows it up?"

"Out on the other side to new cities."

"Where do the leaves in the forest go
when they fall from the trees?"

"Into the ground to become part of new trees with new leaves that will fall again."

"But that is the end of something," the little boy said.
"It is the end of autumn."

"Yes," said his mother, "and the end of autumn is when the winter begins."

"And the end of winter?" asked the little boy.

"The end of winter, when the snow melts and the birds come back, is the beginning of spring," his mother said.

The little boy smiled. "It really does
go on and on," he said. "Nothing ends."
He looked out at the sky. The sun was
gone completely. The lovely pink clouds
had disappeared. The sky was dark and
purple-black. High in the branches of the
pear tree shone, clearly now, a thin new moon.

"Today is over now," the mother said,
tucking him in. "It's time to sleep.
When you wake, the moon will be beginning
another night far away, and the sun
will be here, beginning a new day."